Dear Parent:
Your child's love of re___

Every child learns to read in a different way and at its own speed.
You can help your young reader improve and become more confident
by encouraging his or her own interests and abilities. You can also guide
your child's spiritual development by reading stories with biblical values
and Bible stories, like I Can Read! books published by Zonderkidz. From
books your child reads with you to the first books he or she reads alone,
there are I Can Read! books for every stage of reading:

SHARED READING
Basic language, word repetition, and whimsical
illustrations, ideal for sharing with your emergent reader.

BEGINNING READING
Short sentences, familiar words, and simple concepts for
children eager to read on their own.

READING WITH HELP
Engaging stories, longer sentences, and language play
for developing readers.

READING ALONE
Complex plots, challenging vocabulary, and high-interest
topics for the independent reader.

ADVANCED READING
Short paragraphs, chapters, and exciting themes for the
perfect bridge to chapter books.

I Can Read! books have introduced children to the joy of reading since
1957. Featuring award-winning authors and illustrators and a fabulous
cast of beloved characters, I Can Read! books set the standard for
beginning readers.

A lifetime of discovery begins with the magical words **"I Can Read!"**

Visit www.icanread.com for information on enriching your child's reading experience.
Visit www.zonderkidz.com for more Zonderkidz I Can Read! titles.

Children, obey your parents in the Lord,
for this is right.
—*Ephesians 6:1*

ZONDERKIDZ

Troo's Big Climb
Copyright © 2011 by Cheryl Crouch
Illustrations copyright © 2011 by Kevin Zimmer

Requests for information should be addressed to:
Zonderkidz, *Grand Rapids, Michigan 49530*

Library of Congress Cataloging-in-Publication Data

Crouch, Cheryl, 1968-
    Troo's big climb/ story by Cheryl Crouch ; pictures by Kevin Zimmer.
       p. cm. — (I can read! level 2) (Rainforest friends)
      ISBN 978-0-310-71808-6 (softcover)
      [1. Obedience—Fiction. 2. Tree kangaroos—Fiction. 3. Kangaroos—Fiction.
    4. Rain forest animals—Fiction. 5. Christian life—Fiction.] I. Zimmer, Kevin, ill.
    II. Title.
    PZ7.C8838Tb 2010
    [E]—dc22
    {B}   2009037514

All Scripture quotations, unless otherwise indicated, are taken from the Holy
Bible, *New International Reader's Version*®, *NIrV*®. Copyright © 1996, 1998, by
Biblica, Inc.™ Used by permission of Zondervan. All rights reserved worldwide.

Editor: Mary Hassinger
Art direction & design: Jody Langley

Printed in China

11 12 13 14 15 /SCC/ 10 9 8 7 6 5 4 3 2 1

I Can Read!

READING 2 WITH HELP

RAINFOREST FRIENDS
TROO'S BIG CLIMB

story by Cheryl Crouch

pictures by Kevin Zimmer

Troo stood beside the biggest,
tallest tree in the rainforest.
"I can climb it," he said, "easy."
Rilla said, "To the top?
No way."

Troo looked up.

He looked up some more.

He could not see the top.

Maybe his friend Rilla was right.

Rilla said, "I dare you to try.

I don't think you can do it."

"Sure I can," said Troo.

"I think you are afraid," she said.

Rilla sounded brave and strong.

"You climb it!" Troo said.

"Water rats don't climb, silly!"

said Rilla.

"But tree kangaroos do.

You should be a great climber."

"I am!" Troo said. "I'm the best."

Troo looked at the big tree again.

"My mom told me not to," he said.

"Why?" Rilla asked.

"My mom thinks I am still a baby,"
said Troo.

Troo touched the trunk of the tree.

"My dad also said not to climb it."

"Then don't," Rilla told him.

"Don't they see how strong I am?"
Troo asked.

He started up the tree.

He would show Rilla.

He would show his mom and dad.

Troo loved to feel his arms pulling.

He loved to feel his legs pushing.

He loved to see Rilla getting small

far below him on the ground.

"Ha!" Troo called. "I am not afraid.

I am not a baby.

I am strong!"

Rilla yelled back,

but Troo could not hear her.

"That's another good thing

about climbing!" he said to himself.

Troo looked through the branches.

He saw his family's home.

He stopped smiling.

Would his parents be proud

to see him high in this tree?

15

Well, Troo did not want to stop now.

Up and up he climbed.

His family's tree was far below him.

At last he got to the top branch.

The dry, brown limb stood high

above the tops of the other trees.

Troo looked over

his rainforest home.

He looked at the waterfall.

He looked at the trees and flowers.

He yelled,

"I'm on top of the world!"

SCREECH!

A hawk swooped at him.

Troo saw the bird's sharp claws.

That huge hawk could pick him up

and take him far from his home!

Troo jumped for a lower branch,

but it was dry.

CRACK! It broke.

Down and down Troo fell.

CRASH!

SNAP!

POW!

OOMF!

Troo landed hard on the ground.

He hurt all over.

He could not move.

Rilla screamed, "Are you dead?"

Troo moaned. "Maybe."

Troo's mom and dad came running.

"Are you hurt, Troo?" they asked.

"Yes, but I will be okay," he said.

"Am I in big trouble?"

Troo's dad said, "Yes, son.

God says you should obey us.

You did not obey, and you got hurt."

"This tree is old and dead,"

said Troo's mom.

"It is not safe, even for a

big, strong climber like you!"

Oh! Troo's parents did not think

he was a small, weak baby.

They loved him.

They wanted him to be safe.

Troo said, "I am so sorry.

I will obey now."

Troo's mom kissed his cheek.

"I'll carry you home," said his dad.

Troo smiled at his parents.

He had been to the top of the world,

but home was even better.

Troo

A tree kangaroo with claws and a tail that help him move more easily in trees than on land.

Flame of the Forest

A plant that is used for food, to make medicine, and dye.

Rilla

A water rat who is comfortable on land and in water.

Peacock Spider

A jumping spider. The male has a red, black, and blue belly.

Boyd's Forest Dragon

A lizard found in Australian rainforests. They love to perch on tree trunks all day long.